DON'T FORGET TO CHECK OUT  GREAT HERITAGE PRESS BOOKS:

IF ONLY I HAD WINGS

CHARLIE

MY ALPHABET ANIMALS

LITTLE BIRD, LITTLE BIRD, IT'S TIME FOR BED

LITTLE BIRD, LITTLE BIRD, IT'S TIME TO PLAY

I REMEMBER THE TIME

HERITAGE PRESS

TO JAZMYNN:
Thanks for all the laughs and smiles. :)

It Is NOT Time For Bed

Readers Are Leaders Book Series
An imprint of Heritage Press
Beaverton, Oregon

HERITAGE PRESS

It is **NOT** Time for Bed

"I'm tired," said Ginger.
"Me, too," said Ed.
"I'm grumpy," said Roger.
"It's time for bed."

"It is *NOT* time for bed," said Henrietta.
"We haven't brushed our teeth."

So Ginger and Ed and Roger
and Molly and Ricky and Baxter
and Dolly and Chip...and Henrietta
went down the hall to brush their teeth.

They all squeezed into the bathroom.

"Wait a minute," said Henrietta.
"Wait just one minute."
"Where's Peggy?"

Everyone looked around for Peggy...
...but she was not there.

Henrietta found her.
She was sleeping under her bed.

"Come on, Peggy. You haven't brushed your teeth."

"All done," said Dolly.
"Me, too," said Ed.
"I'm finished," said Ricky.
"It's time for bed."

"It is *NOT* time for bed," said Henrietta.
"We haven't washed our faces."

So Ginger and Ed and Roger
and Molly and Ricky
and Baxter and Dolly
and Chip and Peggy... and Henrietta
grabbed washcloths to wash their faces.

"I'm clean," said Molly.
"Me, too," said Ed.
"I'm fresh," said Baxter.
"It's time for bed."

"It is *NOT* time for bed," said Henrietta.
"We haven't put on our pajamas."

So Ginger and Ed and Roger
and Molly and Ricky
and Baxter and Dolly
and Chip... and Henrietta
went down the hall to their bedroom
to get their pajamas.

"Wait a minute," said Henrietta.
"Wait just one minute."
"Where's Peggy?"

Everyone looked around for Peggy...
...but she was not there.

Henrietta found her.
She was sleeping in the bathroom
under her washcloth.

"Come on, Peggy. You haven't put on your pajamas."

"I'm dressed," said Chip.
"Me, too," said Ed.
"Pj's on," said Ginger.
"It's time for bed."

"It is *NOT* time for bed," said Henrietta.
"We haven't said good night."

So Ginger and Ed and Roger
and Molly and Ricky
and Baxter and Dolly
and Chip... and Henrietta
went to the living room.

"Good night, Dad," said Ricky. He gave his dad a rhino kiss.

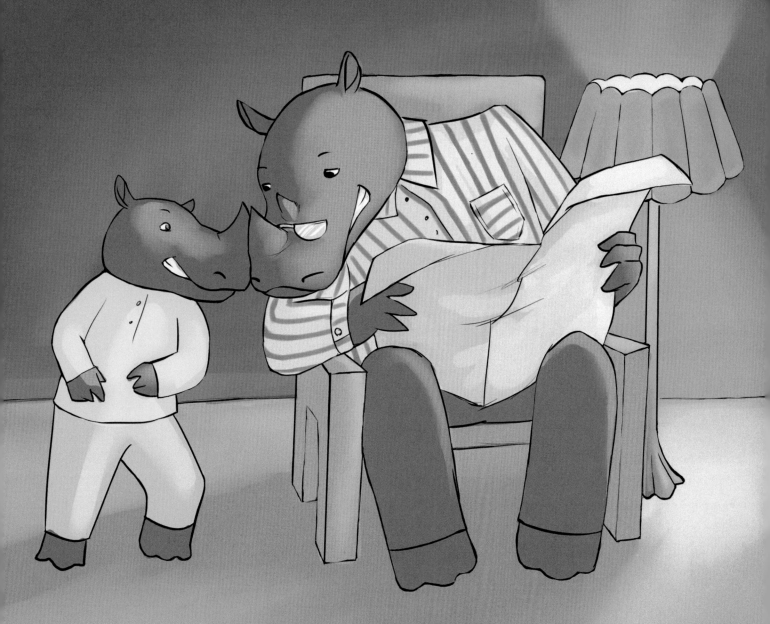

"Good night, Mom," said Baxter. He gave his mom a bear hug.

"Wait a minute," said Henrietta.
"Wait just one minute."
"Where's Peggy?"

Everyone looked around for Peggy...
...but she was not there.

Henrietta found her.
She was sleeping in her dresser drawer.

"Come on, Peggy. You haven't said good night."

"Good night," said Molly.
"Love you," said Ed.
"Sleep well," said Dolly.
"It's time for bed."

"It is *NOT* time for bed," said Henrietta.
"We haven't crawled under our blankets."

So Ginger and Ed and Roger
and Molly and Ricky
and Baxter and Dolly
and Chip... and Henrietta
crawled into their beds.

"What a day," said Ricky.
"That was fun," said Ed.
"Get some rest," said Dolly.
"It's time for bed."

"It is *NOT* time for bed," said Henrietta.
"We haven't turned off the lights."

So Ginger and Ed and Roger
and Molly and Ricky
and Baxter and Dolly
and Chip...and Henrietta
turned off their lights.

"Wait a minute," said Henrietta. "Wait just one minute." "Where's Peggy?"

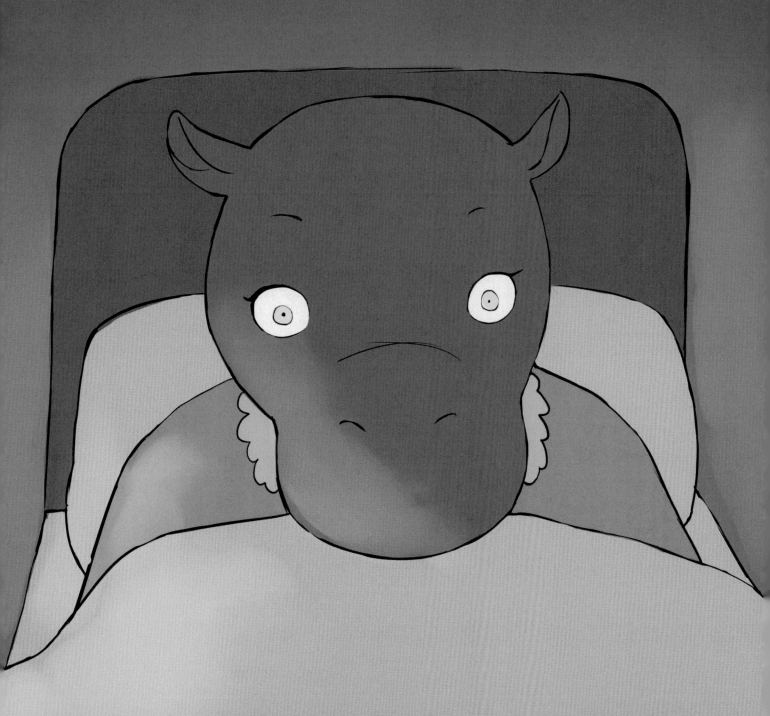

Everyone looked around for Peggy...
...but she was not there, and her light was still on.

Henrietta found her.
She was sleeping under the couch.

"Come on, Peggy. You have to crawl into bed."

"Good night, Peggy," said Ricky.
"Sleep well," said Ed.
"No snoring," said Roger.
"It's time for bed."

"It *IS* time for bed," said Henrietta.
"Good night, Peggy"...

...but Peggy was fast asleep.

my alphabet animals

by Betsie Lewis

Have fun helping your child learn the letters and sounds of the alphabet with My Alphabet Animals.

This fun and adorable children's book will teach all 26 letters of the English alphabet, including the sounds that each letter makes. With carefully chosen animals to represent the primary consonant and vowel sounds, you'll be giving your child a head start for preschool or kindergarten or helping older students finally master the alphabet or phonics as they move forward with learning how to read.

More information available at Amazon.com

Little Bird, Little Bird, It's Time For Bed

Free audiobook included!

It's the end of the day and Oscar the Owl cannot find Little Bird to let him know it's time for bed. His animal friends search for Little Bird before it's dark. Join Oscar the Owl, Frita the Fox, Henry the Hedgehog, Debbie the Deer, Bobby the Bear, Martha the Mouse, Randy the Rabbit, and Sally the Snail as they search for Little Bird.

More information available at Amazon.com

Little Bird, Little Bird, It's Time To Play

Free audiobook included!

It's a playing day and Oscar the Owl plays hide and seek with Little Bird. His animal friends know where Oscar is, but they can't say a word. Do you see Oscar the Owl? (Shhh...)
Play along with Frita the Fox, Henry the Hedgehog, Bobby the Bear, Randy the Rabbit, and Sally the Snail.

More information available at Amazon.com

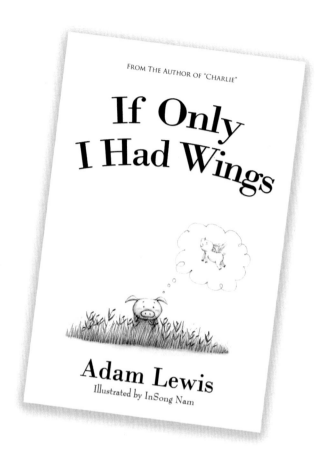

This is an adorable story about realizing how special you are because you're unique!

Susie the piglet has convinved herself that she would be happy if she only had wings. She soon convinces her friends that they they would be happy, too, if they could just have their own set of wings.

Come along with Susie and Chester and Daisy and Pete as they embark on an adventure to find that rooster and get their own set of wings.

Along the way, they'll learn an important life lesson about being unique and special ...and what being a rooster is *really* like.

More information available at Amazon.com

Made in the USA
Middletown, DE
30 June 2017